MATT

I REALLY ENJOYED WRITING THIS BOOK

SQUIRRELS ARE AMAZING CREATURES

OUR GRANDCHILDREN SAY THIS BOOK IS
ABOUT NANCY ANN ME

I THINK THEY MIGHT BE CORRECT

[signature]

D1450344

SQUIRRELLY THE SQUIRREL AND STARLETT

WRITTEN BY **Larry Friend**

ILLUSTRATED BY **Sidney "Mindy" Makis**

outskirtspress

DENVER, COLORADO

Squirrelly the Squirrel and Starlett
All Rights Reserved.
Copyright © 2013 Larry Friend
v4.0 R1.0

Cover images and illustrations © 2013 Sidney Makis. All rights reserved - used with permission.

Outskirts Press, Inc.
http://www.outskirtspress.com

ISBN: 978-1-4327-8658-8

Outskirts Press and the "OP" logo are trademarks belonging to Outskirts Press, Inc.

PRINTED IN THE UNITED STATES OF AMERICA

ACKNOWLEDGMENT PAGE

I would like to thank my wife, Nancy, for instilling in me her love of animals. When we moved to our new home, we were fortunate to acquire five and a half acres of land. On this property are a variety of trees and bushes, as well as several open areas of grass and water. Around our house, Nancy placed many bird and squirrel feeders. After watching the actions and antics of the squirrels and birds living on the property, I was inspired to write this story.

Thank you to my children and grandchildren. They have always been patient with me when I tell them stories. It is from these tales that many of the ideas in the book are derived.

I appreciate all the people who read my many drafts of this story. Your suggestions and recommendations were invaluable. Outside advice and input on any book are extremely important.

I am very pleased to work again with my sister, Mindy Makis. As she did in our first book, *Icy the Iceberg*, she took my written words and brought them to life through her drawings.

Finally, I am fortunate to again have the help of Brian Behling. Through his suggestions, we were able to design the size and shape of the book, as well as what type of drawings would be best suited for the book. When Mindy finished them, he gave us excellent advice as to where they should be placed. He was also very instrumental in designing the front and rear covers.

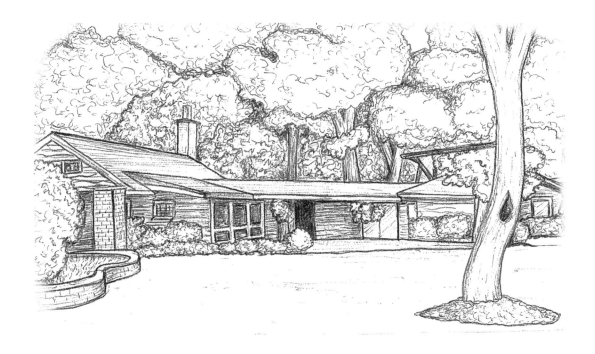

This story takes place on five and a half acres of wooded land in a suburb north of Chicago. There are many grand, tall oak trees on this property. An old log cabin, constructed in 1924, is nestled among the trees. The oak trees were little, but plentiful, when the cabin was constructed. Hence the name of the road in front of the log cabin became Oak Spring Road. Due to the large number of woodchucks during and after construction, the original owner referred to it as Woodchuck Lodge. Many animals and birds make their homes in the trees, plants, and grass. This is a story of one of these families living on this section of the property.

CHAPTER 1
THE NEW FAMILY

One cool spring day a baby boy squirrel was born in the top of a very tall oak tree. After this squirrel entered the world, he was joined by three sisters and one brother.

The parents had built a nest in the top of one of the oak trees. It was constructed of branches, leaves, and grass. The nest was large and, at first, easily held the family of seven. The oak tree was over 100 years old and stood over fifty feet tall. The nest itself was *approximately* forty-five feet above the ground.

Because they had little hair, the babies huddled together to preserve their body heat. They were so cute, but oh so helpless. The mother and father had to do everything for them. The mother nursed them to supply them with nourishment. Both the mother and father had to take turns leaving the nest to eat. Their mother had to *ingest* a considerable amount of food to feed her children. The parents also had to be extremely watchful in order to protect them from predators.

After several weeks, the babies became more self-sufficient. They were able to move about the nest and peer over the side. They were very frightened when they did this because they feared falling out of the nest. Everything looked so small on the ground. They knew they would not survive if they fell from that height.

In a few more weeks the nourishment supplied by the mother was not sufficient to satisfy their hunger. They also noticed that they were getting bigger and the amount of space in the nest grew smaller. At the same time the babies started to be able to talk to one another and their parents. At first they had difficulty understanding each other, but every day it got easier.

As the family grew, the room in the nest became *inadequate*. One day the mother and father gathered the children and advised them that things would have to change. Some of them would remain there, while others would have to move to the winter nest for a period of time. The winter nest was a large hole in the trunk of one of the trees where material had been placed to make it comfortable. This was where the mother and father spent the winter months. The parents decided that the girls would remain in the first nest, where the mother could teach them how to care for it and look for food. The boys would move to the winter location, where their father could teach them how to build another nest, look for food, and protect their family.

CHAPTER 2

MOVING TO THE WINTER NEST

When it was time to move to the new nest, the older brother was terrified. He had been looking over the side of the nest for days. Thoughts of falling down swirled in his head, and he was unable to remove the fear of certain death if he fell from this height. He was positive he would be unable to venture out when it became *mandatory*. His father assured him that he would be able to accomplish this task after some training. His father told him that squirrels possess claws attached to their arms and legs which allow them to climb up and down a tree with no trouble at all. Their father demonstrated how to climb up a branch to the tree trunk and then *descend* head first to another branch.

After several days of instruction and considerable practice, the elder son was able to leave the nest with only slight fear and little effort. It was of some surprise to him that a task that had seemed at first so *daunting* now seemed so effortless. In fact he became more and more fearless. He would run around the nest and hang from the branches under the nest. His father was worried that his actions could lead to his *demise*. After watching him for several days, he viewed him as being a little bit crazy. His father and mother did not want to call him crazy. Therefore, they lovingly gave him the name "Squirrelly."

Squirrelly and his father eagerly taught the rest of the siblings how to exit the tree and reach the ground. This was good because the mother's milk was not sufficient to completely satisfy the rapidly growing young. Everyone knew it was *imperative* that they start looking for nuts and seeds, as well as locating a supply of clean, fresh water.

The father and his sons moved into the winter nest. As would become more and more apparent to Squirrelly, his brother did not like to exert himself. Because the winter nest was only a large hole in a tree, needing little improvement, his brother felt very comfortable there. Also, little sunlight entered the opening, so his brother was able to sleep for long periods of time, *expending* little effort. Often he was content to snooze, curled up in a ball in the corner of the nest, while Squirrelly and his father searched for food. Squirrelly did not like this nest at all. To him it was damp, dark, and dingy.

CHAPTER 3

CONSTRUCTION OF
THE NEW NEST

Feeling more and more like a prisoner in his own home, and becoming increasingly frustrated, Squirrelly finally shouted to his father, "I want to build another nest!" His father replied, "I agree; let's get started immediately!" His father knew it would be necessary for his son to construct a home of his own when he eventually had a family. Therefore, he felt it would be a perfect opportunity, at this early age, to supply him with the necessary training.

After a short period of searching, Squirrelly's father urgently *summoned* him to the top of another tree. He had located a *crotch* in a tree formed by three branches with perfectly shaped *crooks*. Hurriedly, they started constructing the nest. Squirrelly's brother did not like physical labor. He was very content to remain in one place and sleep. Both Squirrelly and his father *admonished* him and demanded that he help them with the work. He would *reluctantly* accompany them, contributing as little effort as necessary.

Squirrelly loved working on the project. He would look for the best twigs, the most beautifully shaped leaves, and the strongest stalks of grass. In the section where he was going to stay, he took extra time to find soft materials such as the fluff on the cottonwood seeds, shredded bark, and the soft ends of grass to *intertwine* with the other construction parts. The final outcome was a very soft area where he could sleep and relax.

Squirrelly, saddened that he had been separated from his mother and sisters, was consumed with a desire to construct a much larger nest. He never again wanted his parents to have to divide future families. This experience was so burned into his memory bank that he knew he would always construct a home big enough to hold any of his future families, no matter how large.

After several weeks, the nest was finished. It was beautiful! Squirrelly, his father, and his brother moved into the new quarters.

Squirrelly was *ecstatic*. The nest was so warm and cozy. During the day he would look at the beautiful clouds in the sky. He was *fascinated* by the large *billowing* white cumulus clouds, appearing as though giant cotton candy puffs were floating above his head. He loved feeling the heat of the sun on his face. The only thing he didn't like was the rain. Everyone, including the nest, got wet. It would take a while for everything to dry out and get warm. At night he would lie on his back and stare at the *magnificent* stars in the sky. The beauty of these sparkling objects amazed him. He loved watching the moon as it changed shapes in the sky. He was very happy.

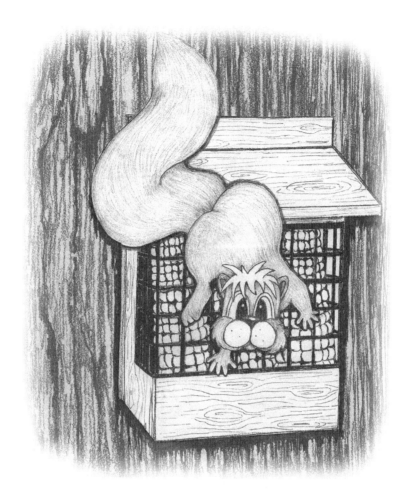

CHAPTER 4
OBTAINING FOOD

Due to the fact that they had devoted so much time to constructing the nest, Squirrelly's father became concerned because they had not acquired and stored enough food. He knew from previous experience that they had to accumulate sufficient food to supply everyone during the winter months. Squirrelly was no longer afraid to ascend or descend the trees. Urgently beginning their quest for food, quickly descending the tree from their nest, they *scurried* into the adjacent yard. To their good fortune, the woman who lived in the log cabin loved birds and animals.

Several times a week she placed dried cereal, dried bread, peanuts in the shell, and special seed mixes outside the house for the squirrels and the chipmunks. She would also put dried cobs of corn in a metal bracket attached to a shag bark black walnut tree. All the other residents in the house as well as their guests were also very kind to the birds and animals. Several times Squirrelly asked his father why they were so fortunate to be born in this area, where there was such a large quantity and variety of foods. His father replied with the only answer he could find acceptable. "Our family is blessed to be here. Always be thankful for this."

During this time, Squirrelly's mother and sisters were reunited with their family in the larger nest. To them, the nest was lovely. They complimented their father and their brothers on its quality and comfort. Everyone was so happy because they were able to cuddle together.

Every day they were now able to exit the nest as a family and enter the yard to acquire food. In addition to the food supplied by the woman of the house, there was always plentiful food under the bird feeders. As the birds ate the seed in the feeders, a percentage of the seed fell on the ground. Some of the birds liked to eat the food on the ground. All of these, especially the mourning doves and mallard ducks, were docile and did not fight with the squirrels over the food. Everyone got along and shared.

It has been said that squirrels are so smart that eventually they can access any feeder. They are very inventive and *ingenious*. This explains the invention of many different types of bird feeders. Complementing this intelligence is their ability to leap up to ten feet from a tree to a feeder. Also, they can hang, using their tails for balance, by their front and back feet. Their gymnastic skills allow them to access feeders from a variety of angles. Once a squirrel is on a feeder it is only a matter of time before he figures out how to defeat it. They never seem to give up trying until they succeed.

Often the squirrel family would look at the bird feeders. They assumed that if they were able to obtain access to these feeders, an even greater supply of food would be available. However, the woman who filled the feeders did not want the squirrels in or on the feeders because they would eat all the bird food. Therefore, she purchased bird feeders that were designed to be "squirrel proof." Some of the squirrels looked at the feeders, viewed them as a *challenge,* and would try everything to defeat them. Others viewed them as an obstacle and would quickly give up.

Squirrelly was very *shrewd*. He learned all the tricks necessary to get into places *inaccessible* to other squirrels. He became the most productive squirrel when it came to *retrieving* food for his family and friends.

Squirrelly was viewed as the "main squirrel." As he got older, everyone expected him to think of ways to beat a new bird feeder. He would watch it, intently study it, and then come up with a method to defeat it. After a day or two he would go into action.

One of the first feeders he *encountered* was designed to hold a large amount of feed. Almost a whole bag of feed could be poured into the middle section. The seed was *dispersed* through small slots next to the middle section. The seeds fell into a tray where the birds could sit on a perch and eat the seeds. However, in front of the slots was a metal flap, which would cover the slots when the weight of a squirrel was placed on the bar. It was then impossible for the squirrel to reach the seed. Squirrelly was able to jump to the top of the feeder from a nearby tree. He would proceed to *slither* down onto its roof. But, the first several times, he fell off the roof of the feeder and landed on the ground. He then learned how to jump from the top cover to the bird perch in front of the feeder. But due to his weight, the bar in front of the feeder would close and he could not reach any of the seed. He would hang on the bar for a short period of time until he again fell to the ground. With more practice he was able to hold onto the edge of the top with his rear feet and stretch his body to reach the seed openings without touching the bar. He could then put one of his paws inside the opening and scoop out a small amount of feed. The seeds would fall to the ground, where his family and friends could eat. He was successful, but the number of seeds recovered were not worth the effort. He decided to leave this feeder alone and try another one in the yard.

In another area of the yard there were two feeders mounted on arms attached to a wooden pole. These were comprised of small *cylindrical* glass tubes about two inches in diameter. At the bottom of the cylinders were two small holes, where the birds could sit on perches to reach the seed. Squirrelly learned that he could pull himself up the pole until he reached the top. He would then climb out one of the arms supporting the feeder until he reached the top of the feeder. His back legs supported his body while he hung down in front of the glass cylinder, reaching the opening in the bottom. He would reach into the opening and pull out feed, which would fall to the ground. He would then return to the ground and eat until he was content. He was very happy with what he had learned. But the woman in the house was not. She yelled at him several times. After this no longer worked, she resorted to using her air horn. She used this horn to *disperse* flocks of birds that *descended* onto her feeders. She also used it to chase away many Canadian geese that entered the yard. The horn was very loud. Squirrelly ran away many times, but, after a while, it no longer bothered him.

After several days, he again climbed the pole. As he approached the feeder, he noticed that the woman had made an addition to the feeder. She had placed two cylindrical wire cages around the feeders. There were small square holes in the cage. The holes were large enough for a small bird to enter the feeder on the inside, but small enough to keep out large birds, raccoons, and squirrels. Squirrelly was puzzled by these. However, after a short period of time, he learned that he could hang on the outer cage, reach inside the opening, grab the cylinder, and shake it *vigorously*. The seed would fall on the ground, where his friends and family could eat them. Apparently, the woman in the house was even more angry because she blew the horn on many more occasions. This made Squirrelly chuckle.

Several days later, when Squirrelly returned to obtain food, he started climbing the pole. However, as he climbed, he noticed it getting darker and darker the higher he climbed. After several feet, his head hit something hard, and he could climb no further. He tried several times with the same result. What was wrong? He decided to back up and *analyze* the problem from a distance. Aha! The woman had attached a large metal tube to the pole. It had an opening at the bottom where an animal could enter, but was closed at the top so there was no exit. The *circumference* of the tube was too large for an animal to get its arms around. No matter how hard he tried, he was unable to climb over or under the tube. *Disgusted*, he decided to move to another feeder that might be easier.

One day, Squirrelly noticed some activity on the other side of the house. He decided to investigate. He became aware of the presence of a worker digging a deep hole outside the woman's office window. After the hole was complete, he dropped in a very tall iron pole with two metal arms on top. He leveled the pole and then poured in several bags of cement to fill the hole. The next day it appeared to Squirrelly that the pole was finished.

Squirrelly was pretty excited. The pole was close enough to a tree from which he could jump on top of the feeder. Consequently, he wondered what type of feeder might be hung on the arms of the pole. He could hardly wait.

The next day the woman came out of the house with a box containing a feeder unlike he had ever seen. She unpacked it, filled it with bird food, and installed two small items in a tube attached to the perch at the bottom of the feeder. The device was a tall glass tube about six inches in diameter, with a large mushroom-shaped dome on the top. She hung the feeder on one of the arms and a flowering plant on the other.

As soon as the woman left, the birds started visiting the feeder. Squirrelly watched many types of birds fly to the feeder, sit on the round perch surrounding the clear tube, and eat seeds from the openings in the bottom. As the birds ate, Squirrelly partook of some of the seeds that fell to the ground.

After *analyzing* the feeding process for a while, Squirrelly came to the conclusion that it was going to be a *cinch* to jump onto the dome from the nearby tree, carefully slide down the plastic surface, grab onto the cylinder, and slowly shimmy down the tube. Finally, sitting on the round perch at the bottom, he would be able to eat until he was full. He even *anticipated* being a hero again as he threw food onto the ground for his fellow squirrels.

He waited for the birds to leave. Now was his chance. He climbed the tree and made a long leap to the top of the dome. He was gleeful. This was going to be a snap. He knew the woman had made every feeder she installed more and more difficult. He figured she had finally make a mistake.

Little did Squirrelly know that the two small items the woman had inserted in the bottom of the feeder were batteries. These batteries powered a motor that would rapidly spin the perch when the weight of a squirrel was detected.

After sitting on top of the dome for several minutes, gloating over his success, Squirrelly slowly descended the tube, landed on the round perch, and started reaching into one hole containing food. But as soon as his weight hit the perch, it began spinning. What was happening? He held onto the wire with his two front paws. The perch was spinning faster and faster! Pretty soon, Squirrelly was spinning so fast that his body was *perpendicular* to the feeder. It got harder and harder to hold onto the perch. After *twirling* around five or six times, going ever faster, he could hold on no longer. He felt himself flying through the air. There was a flagstone walk next to the feeder with a small wall surrounding it. Squirrelly hit the stones and bounced into the wall. He hit his head on the edge of the wall. It really hurt! He saw stars and was unable to breathe. He lay there for several minutes until he regained his breath and was able to start thinking more clearly. He slowly stood up, brushed himself off, and looked at the feeder. Next, turning around and looking into the office window, he was sure he saw the woman laughing at him. He came to the conclusion that she was smarter than he thought. He vowed never to attempt that feeder again. *Disgusted*, he decided to return to the corn feeder.

OBTAINING FOOD

One task that took a lot of time and energy on Squirrelly's part was accessing the corn cobs pressed between the wires of the corn feeder cage. The woman in the house would replace the corn cobs several times a week. This was a great treat for all the squirrels. But the openings in the wire mesh around the corn cobs were small. Squirrelly would have to get into many *contorted* positions in order to break the corn kernels off the cob. It took extreme coordination and *dexterity* between the squirrel's feet and teeth. The seeds would fall to the ground, where everyone would eat them. Squirrelly did not mind doing the work for his family and friends. However, he did get angry when the ducks and chipmunks would eat the food. They could not reach the corn feeder. They would wait under the feeder until Squirrelly did his work and then eat. Because the ducks were large, they would consume a large amount of seed. Squirrelly often had *confrontations* with the ducks. Sometimes the ducks would win, and other times Squirrelly was victorious.

Squirrelly's brother was the direct opposite. He was very lazy and refused to help himself, let alone others. His lack of ambition kept him from taking any action until the seeds fell into an area where he could *retrieve* them. He knew that Squirrelly loved to work and would always make certain there was a continuous supply of food for him. Squirrelly often became angry at his brother's lack of ambition, but he did feel it was not worth a heated confrontation over the situation. The rest of the family truly appreciated his generosity.

CHAPTER 5

FAMILY NAMES ARE ASSIGNED

In the summer, all of the animals were happy. In addition to the squirrel food the residents placed around the house, the falling food from the bird feeders and corn cob cage supplied further *abundance*. This was not a stressful time for the squirrels. In addition to eating, they had time to play, roll around, do somersaults, chase each other, swim in the birdbath, jump from tree branch to tree branch, and run up, down, and around the tree trunks.

It was at this time that the girl squirrels in the family acquired their names, assigned to them by their actions and behaviors. The sister who always waited for the corn under the corn cage became known as Cornelia. The other sister loved nuts. She waited in excited *anticipation* for the woman to put out peanuts. She received the name of Nutella. The other sister enjoyed playing in the birdbath. At the edge of the birdbath there was a statue of a squirrel. She liked pretending that she was playing in the water with one of her imaginary friends. She could even be observed talking to the statue. They assigned her the name of Aquafina.

As their brother did almost nothing, they had a difficult time coming up with a name for him, other than lazy. Many times it appeared that he had the energy of a slug. Therefore his parents *reluctantly* started calling him Sluggo. *Appropriately*, the name stuck.

Squirrelly lived up to his name because he had so much energy and would do many unusual things. He would run up and down the trees, roll over many times, do back flips, and chase his tail for long periods of time. Some of his actions and dance moves made everyone laugh until they had difficulty breathing. He would also venture out into various dangerous locations, not realizing the *consequences*. He would jump from tree limb to tree limb, often coming close to falling from great heights. It was only a matter of time before everyone viewed him as being crazy. More as a matter of affection than reality, they referred to him as Squirrelly rather than Crazy. However, crazy, as his parents had previously thought, would have been more *apropos*.

CHAPTER 6
DANGER LURKS

The young squirrels became *acclimated* to the yard and everything it had to offer. The father decided it was time to give the children further training in additional life experiences. One important lesson was to always be aware of their surroundings. There were several dangerous animals who posed a threat to their well-being. They would try to catch them and eat them. The main predators were hawks, falcons, foxes, and raccoons. During the day it was usually hawks. During the night it was foxes, raccoons, skunks, and sometimes owls. They would try to enter the nests while the family members were sleeping and eat them. However, of all the predators, the ones most feared by the father were the hawks. They would swoop down without warning, grab a squirrel with their talons, and then fly away in an instant. The birds also feared the hawks. Whenever they saw a shadow of a hawk on the ground as it was circling in the sky, they would take cover in the branches of the trees or their nests until the threat had passed. The squirrels were not quite as observant. The father told them to be ever so cautious and watch for the behavior of the birds and chipmunks. If no birds were at the feeders, usually there was a reason to be *vigilant*.

Squirrelly and his sisters listened to their father. No matter what they were doing, either at work or play, they were always on "pins and needles." They had set up a system of warning each other if they sensed danger. They had developed a secret squeaking sound, recognized by all the family members. This sound was similar to the squeaking noise emitted by chipmunks when they become fearful, scurrying from nest to nest. As soon as the danger warning was heard, they would take several evasive actions. Some of them would cling to the side of a tree, not moving, trying to blend in with the bark. Others would find cover under the dense bushes or run into a nearby downspout. They would return to eating as soon as the danger appeared to subside.

Squirrelly's brother paid no attention to his father's instructions. He took no part in learning the group distress calls, showing no desire to give or receive responses. He never *scurried* for cover when danger was present and a warning was issued. He was more interested in feeding himself under the corn cage as Squirrelly worked *diligently* above him, removing corn from the cobs. Squirrelly, being so kind, never complained about feeding his brother.

One day, Sluggo, *gorging* himself as usual and paying no attention to the lack of birds, not listening to the warning calls from his family or the piercing squeaks from the chipmunks, was startled by a sound close to him. Seemingly out of nowhere, a hawk swooped down, latched onto Sluggo, accelerated into the air, and disappeared as quickly as he had appeared. Sluggo was never seen again. The rest of the family was shocked. They were sad at his disappearance. Even with all his faults, he was still a member of their family. They all loved him and were certain, if he had not been taken from them so quickly, they might have been able to change his ways for the better. Still, since he contributed nothing in the way of assistance to the family, his absence was not felt in the area of physical labor. However, it was a lesson learned that would stick with them for the rest of their lives, making them ever more *vigilant*. It would be even more devastating if another member of the family was lost.

CHAPTER 7
SUMMER TURNS INTO FALL

During the summer months, nuts and seeds started appearing on the developing trees.

The cottonwood trees produced fluffy white seeds. They flew everywhere and settled in every nook and crevice. The seeds were too small for the animals to eat, but the fluffy material made great bedding.

The oak trees produced acorns. Starting to develop in May and June, they were ready for consumption in a green tart state in July and August. Preferring to eat the acorns when they matured into a brown and dried state, the squirrels would wait until October or November, after they fell to the ground, to chew on them. Although very tasty and filling, a large percentage of the acorns were buried for food and nourishment, essential during the long, cold winter months.

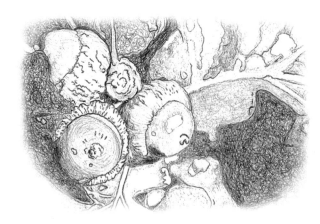

The black walnut trees produced nuts in June, July, and August. The squirrels ate the young, partially developed fruit in the trees. There was a thick, semi-porous green coating around each one. This coating had to be removed before reaching the hard interior and its meat. Considerable effort was necessary, but it was worth all the toil. During this time of year, many squirrels climbed high in the walnut trees to access the nuts. As they removed the outer coverings with their little razor-sharp teeth, the small chipped pieces fell to the ground. In the reflected sunlight these simulated rain. Later in the year these nuts dropped to the ground. Then the green covering started rotting, acquiring a dark brown, almost black color. The squirrels could reach them and their delicious meat with little effort. These were also buried, although less frequently.

The maple trees produced seeds that were smaller than the acorns or black walnuts, but were much more plentiful. Appearing in large groups at the ends of the branches, the seeds, attached by a small stem, had a large wing at one end. These wings allowed the seeds to fly in the wind when detached from the branch. As a bird or a glider flies in air currents, the movement of these seeds transported them to other parts of the land, where new seedlings would appear, eventually developing into new trees. The squirrels found these seeds to be very tasty, both in the *succulent* green state in the summer as well as a dried brown state in autumn. While attached to the twigs in the trees, these seeds were very difficult to access. The ends of the branches were so small that they could barely support the weight of a squirrel. A squirrel had to be experienced to venture out on these limbs.

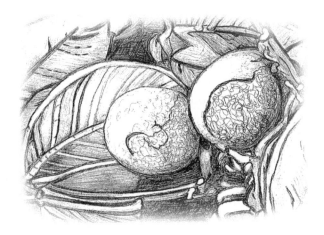

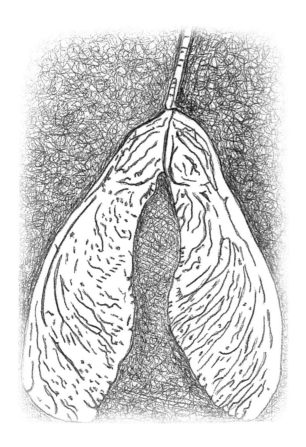

Only training would supply one with the knowledge necessary to *differentiate* between a branch that could support a squirrel and one that could not. With repetition a squirrel would learn to maintain his balance while on a tiny, rapidly bending branch.

One day Squirrelly noticed some squirrels balanced on mere twigs, eating the maple seeds. He asked his father how he, too, could accomplish this task. His father explained that it would take considerable effort to be as good as these squirrels, but he would explain the procedure. First, climbing the main trunk, venturing out on one of the larger branches, and arriving at the tip of a small branch, a squirrel would start to feel it bending under his weight. Then, using every means at his disposal, including his feet, legs, and tail, he would have to balance himself at the end of one or two small branches as he ate the seeds.

As Squirrelly had overcome his fear of climbing up and down trees, he was able to jump from tree to tree and from branch to branch. He felt quite confident that he could now tackle a more difficult *challenge*. Pursuant to his father's instructions, he quickly climbed the maple tree, ventured out on a large branch, and carefully *shimmied* out on the *progressively* smaller branches. He had just reached a large clump of maple seeds when he abruptly lost his balance. He fell to the ground. Fortunately, a maple tree is not as high as a fully grown, lofty oak. Even at this distance, he hit the ground with a loud thump. IT HURT! All the squirrels in the area quickly turned in the direction of the sound. As soon as they realized that Squirrelly was okay, they started laughing and making fun of him. In this instance the pain of their *ridicule* was far worse than the pain he experienced when he collided with the earth. It was at this time that his embarrassment led to a little bit of anger, which then led to an overwhelming desire to succeed in this venture. Each time he fell, he was ridiculed. Each time he became more determined. With this determination, after only nine or ten tries, Squirrelly was able to conquer this task. He was very proud of himself. He had overcome another one of his fears and acquired another life-improving skill. But from then on, he never laughed at anyone for failing at something they had attempted. He knew how hurtful someone's ridicule felt.

CHAPTER 8
STARLETT

The summer progressed and Squirrelly grew older. He was using all the skills he had learned while in the presence of his father and the older, more experienced squirrels. He was thankful every time he saw the woman in the house fill the bird feeder, the corn feeder, and scatter squirrel feed around the yard. He again pondered why he, his family, and friends were so blessed.

Daily, because of the abundance of food, everyone had time to play. Chasing each other around the tree trunks, running up and down the trees, playing hide and seek around the bushes, jumping from tree to tree, splashing in the birdbath, and wrestling on the lawn occupied hours of their time. Periodically, a group of squirrels would grab a little stick. Running and throwing the stick between each other, it appeared as though they were playing a game of squirrel football. What great fun!

One day Squirrelly was chasing one of the squirrels from a neighboring nest. After tiring of this, he decided to return to the corn cage and retrieve more corn. He started diligently working. After several minutes, he became aware of a squirrel on the ground eating the corn. This was the same squirrel with whom he had been playing several days before. At that time this one had appeared different to him. He knew he had had unusual feelings while in the presence of this squirrel. He decided to investigate the *aforementioned* one more closely. He left the corn cage and climbed to the ground to get a closer look. He was right! When he viewed her more closely, she was, to him, unlike any other squirrel with whom he had associated. She had the cutest red ears, with tiny tufts of hair at the ends. She had the most beautiful eyelashes. Her body was sleek and smooth. Every hair on her fur coat was well groomed. She had a magnificent tail. But the thing he noticed most was her eyes. They were so large and dark. To him her eyes sparkled like the stars in the night sky. He couldn't stop looking at them. It was at this time that he began calling her Starlett.

After she left, he could not get her out of his mind. As he thought more about it, he realized that she had been in his presence many times in the past. Whether at work or play, he had enjoyed her company. But, until now, the impression she made on him was no different than those received from other squirrels. Now, as his *perception* of her changed, he wondered if the fact that she was spending so much time around him implied that she also had different feelings about him. Boy, he sure hoped so!

CHAPTER 9
FALL TURNS INTO WINTER

Squirrelly was really enjoying his life. Every day was a new adventure. Because he was having so much fun, time passed very quickly.

As the weeks passed, Squirrelly realized that there was less and less daylight. He noticed that the temperature became colder and colder each day. This made him slightly sad because he had fewer hours to play with his friends.

Squirrelly's father had told him that these changes were going to happen. His father had explained that during this time, a season he had heard people call Winter, there might be times when it would be impossible to leave his nest to search for food. There might be days or weeks before he could find something to eat. During these days of *inclement* weather, he would have to curl up in a ball in his nest and sleep to preserve his body heat.

Because of his father's descriptions, as well as an inner voice warning him of the *impending* danger, he developed an urgent desire to gain weight. He ate more and more food. In fact, it seemed as though his entire day was spent searching for, locating, and eating edible items. Those *cherished* play times had ended.

For some reason, he had a "sixth sense" that told him he would have to gain sufficient fat to protect him during the upcoming winter. He ate more and more and became fatter and fatter. He noticed that all his friends and family were "packing on the ounces." Although Starlett was also gaining weight, she still looked beautiful to Squirrelly. He only wished they had more time to spend with each other.

It was at this time Squirrelly realized that it was time for him to move from the family's nest to a nest of his own. He was aware that a squirrel family had recently vacated a small nest in one of the trees near his family's present nest. They had moved because it was too small for their growing family. However, it was a perfect size for him and one other squirrel. That evening he informed his family of his intention to move out. It was both a happy and sad situation. They knew they would miss all the contributions he had made to the family. But they also realized it was time for him to venture out on his own. They were all proud of him and wished him success. After a tearful good-bye, he departed.

One day, after he had returned, very tired, to his new residence, he fell asleep. Upon waking, he became aware that it was very dark and cold in his nest. He was covered in a white substance. He went to the edge of his nest and peered over the side. What was this material? It was white, fluffy, and cold. It must be snow. Still falling and *glistening* in the sunlight, it appeared as though glitter were dropping from the sky. Squirrelly did not know what to do. He was amazed at the sight. The snow covered everything. He started to dig at it with his little feet and wet nose. He ventured out on one of the branches. All the tree branches were covered. The white fluff concealed the bird feeders, the squirrel cage, and the birdbath. It was beautiful but a little bit scary. How was he going to locate his favorite places for food? Where were his friends? Where was Starlett? When would he be able to see and play with them again?

He decided to venture out on one of the limbs in order to investigate the situation further. He slowly pushed the snow off the branch and carefully inched out. Not only was the snow cold, but it was very slippery. After advancing several feet, he was no longer able to acquire *traction* and keep his balance. He fell from the tree. He remembered falling several times before. He said to himself, "THIS IS GOING TO HURT!" He hit the ground. He felt no impact and heard no thump. It was like falling onto a fluffy white blanket. He was surprised by his lack of pain. But he was also startled when he began sinking into the snow and was quickly covered by it.

He couldn't see anything, and it was almost impossible to breathe. With some urgency, he sensed that he had to dig quickly to the top in order to get a breath of fresh air and obtain his bearings. He rapidly used his front feet, back feet, his tail, and his nose to climb to the surface. When he reached the surface and was able to assess the situation, he was *astonished*. The substance glistened in the sunlight. It was so soft. Because his fur had been growing longer and thicker over the last several weeks, he did not feel cold. As he kept sinking into the snow, it was difficult to move around, but it was a lot of fun. He would dig tunnels under the snow until he needed air and then would quickly return to the surface. He played like this for several hours.

One time when he came up for air, he was surprised to see Starlett in front of him. She, too, was having fun. She looked so cute to him. Snow covered her ears and head. Due to a covering of snow, her eyelashes appeared even larger and longer. Her nose was shiny from the melting snow. Her eyes glistened as the rays of the sun reflected in them. She and Squirrelly played for two or three additional hours. As it started to get dark, they realized that they would have to return to their nests for warmth and protection.

As Squirrelly returned to his nest, he was very cautious. He remembered how slippery the branches had been. It was dark by the time he reached home. He was extremely weary. He immediately curled up in a ball and tried to go to sleep. Before he went to sleep, he had time to think. Squirrelly now understood why his family had moved to a winter nest. These nests were usually located in large holes in the trunk of a large tree. Such a location offered protection for the family that was not found in an open nest in the top of a tree. He knew he would have to start searching for better living quarters in the morning. After a while, he drifted off to sleep.

Even though he was still very tired, early the next day he started his quest for a nest suitable for the rest of the winter. He searched for many hours. He found a large hole in the trunk of a massive oak, but when he tried to enter, he was startled to find it occupied by another family. He found several holes near the base of other trees. These holes would make a very convenient home by providing easy access and no climbing. Remembering his father's warnings about predators, he realized these holes would also provide easy access for them. He took a pass on these openings.

He was about to give up for the day when he noticed a hole just above the branch of a large oak tree. He felt it would be perfect. Not only was it high in the tree, but it was close to his present nest. When he investigated this opening, he found it quite adequate for his needs. It was large enough to hold two or three squirrels. He immediately moved into this nest. As he was now exhausted, cold, and wet, he quickly fell asleep and slept longer than usual. It was not as comfortable as his other nest, but he knew he could remain there until spring, at which time he could construct a nest of his own, using all the skills acquired from his father.

After several days of sleeping, he awoke and slowly crawled to the entrance to evaluate his situation. He noticed that it had gotten much colder, much windier, and there was much more ice. His father's instructions and recommendations regarding winter returned to him. He was thankful he had gained weight and was able to survive without any intake of food. He was able to eat the snow to obtain water. He came to the realization that the less he moved around, the less energy he exerted and the less hungry he became. He just kept sleeping.

CHAPTER 10

THE NPS IS CREATED

It seemed like an eternity before the weather got better. Squirrelly became weary of sleeping curled up in a ball in the corner of his nest. He was very lonely and missed his friends and family. He really missed Starlett. But what could he do? He was afraid, and feared that if he left the nest, he would freeze to death.

After about a week the weather improved. He decided to venture out. He was VERY HUNGRY! He still could not see the bird feeders or the corn cage, and there were no nuts or maple seeds in the trees. He looked for the woman in the house to see if she was going to spread some food on the snow. He saw no one and no food. However, when he looked at the log cabin, he was amazed at the beauty of the icicles hanging from the edge of the roof. Being constructed of frozen water derived from the melting snow on the roof, they glistened in the sun like diamonds. As there were so many of them so closely spaced, coming to sharp, jagged points, it appeared as if they were a hawk's talons ready to grasp its prey as it descended from the sky. He remembered his father warning him about searching for food under these *spear*-like objects. If one of them broke off, there was a distinct possibility that he could be *impaled* by one. He became ever more cautious when near them. He pondered what Sluggo would have done, if still alive, in response to this lesson.

He knew now that he would have to rely on the nuts he had buried during the summer months. One of the lessons his father had taught him was not to eat all the nuts and seeds he had found during the summer. He told Squirrelly to bury some of them so he would have a food supply during the long, cold, snowy winter months. Because there were so many oak trees on the property, there was an ample supply of acorns. Their hard, smooth, wax-like shells, which provided them with the ability to resist water, made them ideal nuts to deposit in the earth. He had buried many acorns and walnuts during the summer.

He knew he would have sufficient food until the snow melted if he could locate the nuts. When he was burying the nuts, he had devised a system of remembering their location. He had developed a mental storage map and a nut positioning system (NPS). This nut positioning system was dependent on reference points in relation to his nest, trees, buildings, etc. He located his first reference point and started counting the paces to the next position. It was hard work! He could work only a limited amount of time under the snow. Often, he had to come up for air. After many attempts, he was not able to locate a single nut. He became more and more frustrated. Due to his extreme hunger and the knowledge that if he did not find food he would starve to death, he knew he could not give up. He told himself, "Calm down and think!" He went over the items one by one, over and over. He thought and meditated. He meditated and thought some more. What was wrong? Had he remembered the directions incorrectly? Had another squirrel eaten the nuts? After what seemed an *eternity*, his stomach grumbling loudly, he suddenly had an *epiphany*. AHA! He was confused by the snow. He was starting his search from the wrong direction. He immediately started tunneling from the opposite direction. He was so excited when he located his first nut. He was surprised at how well preserved it was after spending several months under the cold, wet earth and snow. It was still smooth and *succulent*. Now his NPS worked perfectly. He located nut after nut. He ate until his hunger subsided and felt so much better.

One time, when he came up for air, he was startled by Starlett, who was directly in front of him. She looked extremely cold and very hungry. Squirrelly told her to wait. He quickly dug to his next nut position. He retrieved a nut, carried it through the snow, and presented it to Starlett. She quickly ate it. He did this several more times until she seemed better.

Squirrelly decided to teach her the NPS. He gave her a brief explanation, and she seemed impressed with his intelligence. He asked her to assist him. He would recall the directions and call them out to Starlett. She would locate the nut, and they would share it. They became a great team. Squirrelly soon realized he was much happier and productive with her in his presence. They continued to work together and gained some of the weight they had lost while sleeping for extended periods in their nests.

CHAPTER 11
THE PROPOSAL

Squirrelly kept spending more and more time with Starlett. He never got tired of talking to her as they worked together searching for food. They would help each other tunnel in the snow, blindly search for a nut, grab the nut, and then drag it to the surface. When they reached the top of the snow pile, gasping for air, they would each eat a portion of the nut.

After several weeks, Squirrelly realized that whatever task, no matter how difficult, was less *daunting* when they tackled it together. Every moment in Starlett's presence was *cherished*. It became more and more difficult for them to leave each other at the end of the day, as they returned to their respective nests. Starlett was less lonely because she still lived with her parents. The loneliness was much more severe for Squirrelly. He lived alone, and each day he became more and more depressed when he returned, without his daily companion, to his empty nest. He would sit alone in his favorite chair, staring at the stars, finally falling asleep and then dreaming about Starlett. One evening, he began *reminiscing* about how happy his parents seemed during their years of marriage. He felt it might be time to ask Starlett to marry him. He drifted into a gentle slumber *contemplating* this.

He woke up early the next day. It was still dark outside, so he had time to sit and think about Starlett for several hours. He knew he had to come up with something special before he made his marriage proposal. He pondered and pondered. He knew acorns and corn were her favorite foods. He decided to incorporate these two items when he "popped the question."

During their search for food that day, he was on the lookout for the most beautiful acorn he could find. He finally found one and hid it behind a tree. He then proceeded to search for a shiny, bright yellow, and perfectly shaped kernel of corn. Luckily, he was successful! Later that afternoon he *retrieved* these two items and carried them back to his nest. After he placed the acorn in the middle of his home, he made a slight *indentation* in the top of the acorn and placed the kernel of corn in the hollowed-out space. He then stood back to admire his work. It looked good, but he felt it needed a little more *pizzazz*. Before dark, he returned to the corn feeder and carried back several more kernels of corn. He placed them around the acorn. He again examined his work. He was elated. Everything was perfect!

He could barely wait until the next day. He was so excited to see Starlett in the morning. While they worked together, he found it more and more difficult to contain his emotions. After several hours of hard work, they had some time to play. During his playtime he finally blurted out, "Starlett, would you like to come back to my nest for dinner before you return home for the evening?" He was overjoyed when she said yes.

Toward evening they returned to Squirrelly's abode. When Starlett entered, she noticed the large, perfectly shaped acorn with the shiny golden piece of corn on it. It was beautiful. She asked Squirrelly what it was for. He was a little bit shy, a little bit embarrassed, a tiny bit nervous, and slightly tongue tied. But he *mustered* up the courage, got down on one knee, and said, "Starlett, I cherish every moment that I am with you. I miss you every night when I am alone in my nest. Would you please marry me? I want us to spend the rest of our lives together."

Starlett was very surprised. She had been hoping that Squirrelly would ask for her paw in marriage. But she had no indication that it would happen so soon. She really liked Squirrelly. She wanted to spend more time with him. She was growing weary of returning to her parents' home each evening. After thinking about his proposal for several minutes, Starlett blurted out, "Yes! On two conditions. I want to get married in the next several days, and I want to move in with you within the next week or two."

Squirrelly couldn't believe what he was hearing. Wow! He got up from his one-kneed position, jumped into the air, and gave Starlett a big hug and a kiss.

Together, they both ate the acorn and corn. When finished they talked for a brief period. Then Starlett ran home to break the news to her parents.

Starlett's parents were overjoyed that Squirrelly had chosen to marry her. They always liked Squirrelly and knew she would have a good future with him. The ceremony took place two days later.

For the rest of the winter, Squirrelly and Starlett remained in the nest. When the weather permitted, they would venture out to obtain more food. When the weather was really *inclement*, they would curl up in the nest and sleep. The more time they spent together, the more Squirrelly liked her. Starlett was a perfect companion. She would intently listen to him whenever he talked. And, of course, Squirrelly loved to listen to her concerns and opinions. They talked at length about many things. She would comfort him when he became worried or depressed. She kept the nest clean and organized, even though it was not the exact type of nest he *ultimately* wanted to provide for his family.

CHAPTER 12

A NEW NEST, NEW DREAMS, AND A NEW FAMILY

One of the things Squirrelly appreciated most about Starlett was her ability to share and support his dreams. He could not stop dreaming about their future. He never stopped talking about their life together. They both wanted to have a family. Starlett had been a great help to her mother and her father, as well as a caretaker for her siblings. Now that she was living with Squirrelly and the weather prevented her from leaving their nest for any length of time, she increasingly longed to see her family. Squirrelly also *yearned* to talk to his parents and sisters. He even missed his brother. Even though Squirrelly had to work extra hard to assist Sluggo while he was living, he wished he had not been taken from them. He hoped his sons would not be so lazy. This absence of friends and relatives *accelerated* his and Starlett's desire to establish a family of their own.

Squirrelly had big dreams about the nest he was going to construct for his family.

Sometimes Starlett tired of hearing his plans. But she knew how determined he could be when he got something in his mind. He told her that as soon as the weather improved, he was going to start construction of their new home. He explained what type of tree he was going to search for and how the nest was going to be built. He desired to locate a *crotch* containing three branches with perfect *crooks* to support their nest. Such a strong base should also provide ample protection from high winds. He was going to build a separate section in the nest for Starlett and himself. This area would be much smoother, softer, and more private than the rest of the nest. It would be constructed with the intention of easily holding a family of six or seven children. Starlett seemed excited when he described it to her. He did not mind giving her the best; he knew she would take care of any home he provided.

In March the weather broke. It was beautiful. The days were longer, and the sun shone brighter. The warmth seemed to *rejuvenate* everyone. Squirrelly and Starlett acquired "spring fever." They were absolutely in love. Due to his lack of activity during the winter, Squirrelly had lots of built-up energy. He knew it was time to stop dreaming about the family's nest and start constructing it. He became aware that all the other animals and birds were acting in the same way. There was a bustle of activity among all of them to build nests and locate mates. In April, the trees started to bud and show signs of life.

Squirrelly started searching for the perfect tree. There were many *magnificent*, tall oak trees on the property. After several days, he came across exactly what he was looking for. It was an oak tree about sixty feet tall. There was a crotch with three branches, furnishing a base for a large nest. Due to the presence of many other oak trees surrounding his prospective tree, he was certain it would be shielded from wind as well as partially sheltered from the rain.

The only drawback was the distance of the new location. It was far from their present living quarters. He explained to Starlett that he would have to leave before dawn and return late in the evening. Until the nest was finished, Starlett should look for food while he worked. The food could be brought back to the nest. He would eat when he returned from a long day of labor. He worked on the nest for two weeks. Many of the lessons learned from his father were helpful. He looked for the best sticks and twigs. He *interwove* them to make the nest strong but *resilient*. He found the softest leaves, grass, and shredded bark. He lined the entire nest with cottonwood fluff. Additional padding was added where he and Starlett would sleep.

While working on the nest, he started to observe a noticeable change in Starlett. She seemed to have less energy. She still worked hard, but took more time to rest. Also, she was gaining more weight. At first, Squirrelly was worried. He talked to his mother and father when he met them on one of his trips to the new location. They told him not to worry. From his descriptions, they *perceived* that she was going to have babies.

Squirrelly could not contain himself. He proceeded to jump around, doing flips and somersaults while kicking his little feet together. He kept saying over and over to himself, "Starlett and I are going to have a family!"

He immediately ran home to tell Starlett. She was even more excited than Squirrelly. Since he had just finished the new nest, he decided it was a perfect time to take her there. When they arrived, she was overcome by its beauty. She could not believe that Squirrelly could construct something so *exquisite*.

Since the new dwelling was so strong, smooth, and soft, Starlett felt very comfortable in it. She asked Squirrelly if they could move into the nest that night. As he had just placed the finishing touches on it several hours before, he told her yes. He went out and found some special nuts and seeds. He went to the corn cage and brought back some of the best corn kernels They ate that night in their new home under the light of the moon and stars. After eating, they curled up next to each other and stared at the night sky. Since Squirrelly did not have to leave before dawn this day, they slept until the sun came up. Squirrelly was very pleased with his present circumstances and grateful for everything life had offered him up to this date.

CHAPTER 13
A SEVERE STORM

One night, several weeks after moving, while lying in their new home, Squirrelly and Starlett noticed bright lights flashing in the distance. They also heard large booming noises after the light appeared. This had happened to them several times while growing up. The *consequences* had been minor. There was usually some wind and rain; they would huddle in the nest until it passed. Everyone and everything would get wet. Nonetheless, after a brief drying-out period, things would return to normal.

This time it seemed different to them. The lightning was much more frequent and much more intense. The thunder was louder and more threatening. The storm crept ever closer. The wind picked up. The rain was so heavy that the water started rising inside the nest. Squirrelly and Starlett knew they did not have sufficient time to seek better shelter. Although extremely fearful, Starlett knew that Squirrelly had *invested* considerable effort while constructing the nest. She was confident it would survive such a *devastating* storm. They only hoped and prayed that the supporting branches

were strong enough to prevent them and their home from being blown out of the tree.

As the storm *intensified*, Squirrelly worried more and more about their home as well as Nutella's. It was at this time that Squirrelly remembered a previous wind storm that had blown the nest of Nutella and her mate, Rocky, out of a tree. They were lucky because they had been able to quickly exit their dwelling and cling to the tree's main trunk just before the nest was blown to the ground. After the storm *subsided*, Nutella and Rocky went to the ground searching for *remnants*. After a while, they located their nest. It was *intact*, but was lying in a hole in the ground. WHAT WERE THEY GOING TO DO? Then, Nutella remembered how well Squirrelly had constructed the family nest with their father when they were smaller. She immediately searched for Squirrelly. After locating him, she asked him if he would help them reconstruct the damaged nest in a similar manner. As was his custom, Squirrelly was more than willing to assist them. He spent several days *disassembling* the nest on the ground and carrying the parts piece by piece to the original place in the tree. He reassembled and strengthened it with new materials until he was completely satisfied. Nutella and Rocky were very pleased and extremely *appreciative*.

However, his thoughts of Nutella were only in his mind for a brief moment. Suddenly, a large bolt of lightning hit the tree next to theirs. POW! The light was unbearable and the sound was deafening. BOOM! In an instant, the flash ignited a portion of an adjacent tree. The tree burst into flames and split into two parts, one part crashing onto the ground and the other part hitting the tree containing Squirrelly's nest. The tree shook, the branches whipped, the leaves fell to the ground, and the nest swayed and bounced violently. Luckily, everything remained in one piece and stayed securely stuck in the crotch of the tree. Both Squirrelly and Starlett feared they would not survive the violence.

The storm passed as rapidly as it had started. After the wind and the rain stopped, the moon and stars began to peek through the clouds. Squirrelly and Starlett began to assess the damage. With much gratitude, they found everything okay. Starlett complimented Squirrelly on his building skills. They now knew that the nest would be a wonderful, safe place to raise their family.

Several days later, while out gathering food, Squirrelly came in contact with Nutella. They discussed the storm. Nutella *profusely* thanked Squirrelly for his help in reconstructing their nest. No damage had been sustained. She informed him that she and Rocky were certain they would not have survived such extreme *turbulence* in their old residence. Due to the fact that the storm had appeared so quickly, they were positive they would not have had sufficient time to exit and seek shelter. Squirrelly was their hero. Squirrelly, never boastful, shrugged off the compliment and voiced his thankfulness that Nutella and her family had survived.

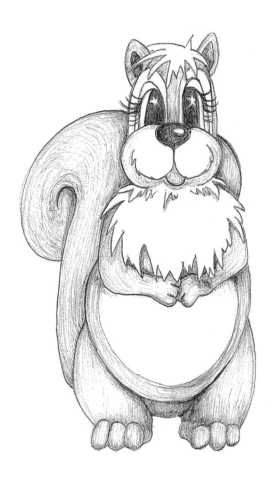

CHAPTER 14

THE NEW FAMILY

Starlett kept getting bigger. It was hard for her to leave the nest. Each day Squirrelly would exit and obtain food for her. Her hunger was *insatiable*. This continued for several weeks. One day, when she seemed to be in considerable pain, Squirrelly tried to console her, but to no avail. After about an hour she gave birth to seven babies, four girls and three boys. The babies were so cute and adorable. Squirrelly was *ecstatic*.

Several hours later, while Squirrelly was lying next to Starlett as she nursed the babies, he started thinking how he was going to raise their family. He was very happy with his life. He was very thankful he had met Starlett. He wanted to give his children the same training and experience he had received from his mother and father. He wanted to be there to calm their fears just as his father had.

He looked forward to watching his family grow and develop. He was so excited that he started telling Starlett what he had planned for the future. She loved his stories, plans, and dreams. She rolled her big, beautiful brown eyes and put on her "listening" ears, knowing it was going to be a long night.

CHAPTER 15
AN UNCERTAIN FUTURE

Life is *unpredictable*. Only time reveals the outcome. However, with the love and companionship of a perfect mate, the ability to face all challenges together without complaining, the desire to work hard, unselfishly helping one another, and the desire to proceed forward with a positive mental attitude, the chances of success are very high.

I am very confident that Squirrelly, Starlett, and their family will have a long, loving, and wonderful life. DO YOU AGREE?

CHAPTER 16
THE FUTURE GENERATION

As the children of Starlett and Squirrelly grew older and were able to leave the nest, they started drawing pictures on leaves. Squirrelly saved these sketches. Is the artwork of each an indication of what their future will hold?

Carlie - Age: 10

Matt - Age: 9

Jessie - Age: 7

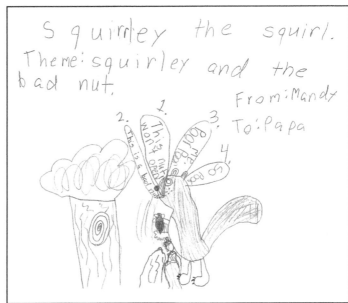

Mandy - Age: 6

Marty - Age: 6

Josh - Age: 3

Hayley - Age: 2

GLOSSARY - SQUIRRELLY
THE SQUIRREL

abundance   Overflow of quantity or supply, large amount

accelerated   To cause to move faster

acclimated   To become used to a new climate or situation

admonished   To warn gently

aforementioned   Mentioned earlier, named before

analyze   To examine critically, study

anticipate   Realize beforehand, expect something ahead of time

appreciative   To be grateful for

appropriately   Suitable for a particular purpose, correctly

approximately   To come near, almost

apropos   Being to the point

astonishment   To be filled with sudden and great wonder

billowing   To rise or roll like rising smoke

challenge   Call to engage in a contest of skill, call to battle

cherished   To hold or treat as dear, cling fondly to, loved

cinch   A sure or easy thing

circumference   The outer boundary of a circle

confrontations   To meet face to face with defiance and opposition

GLOSSARY

consequence	Logical conclusion
consequences	That which so follows, the effect or result of an action
consumption	The using up of goods, eating
contemplating	To look at or view with continued attention, thinking about a conclusion
contorted	Twist body into unusual shapes
coordination	To arrange movements in orderly manner
crook	A curved part on a branch
crotch	Angle formed by parting of two or three branches
cylindrical	Round tube
daunting	Disheartening, overwhelming, difficult
demise	Death
descend	Moving from higher to lower, go down
detected	Discover the presence of, feel something
devastating	To lay to waste, ravage, destroy
dexterity	Skill in using hands and body
differentiate	To perceive or see the difference between, tell apart
diligently	Constant effort and desire to accomplish something
disassembling	To take apart
disgusted	To be offensive to, not to one's liking
disperse	To scatter, spread out, let out
ecstatic	Characterized by delight, very happy

encountered	To come upon, meet with
epiphany	The sudden appearance of an idea, to realize
eternity	Seemingly endless period of time, very long time
exhausted	To use up completely, totally worn out
expending	Using up
exquisite	Of peculiar beauty or charm, elegant, beautiful
fascinated	Enchanted, cast under a spell
glistening	Sparkling, glittering
gorging	To eat greedily, to stuff to capacity
impaled	To be pierced with a pointed object
imperative	Necessary
inaccessible	Difficult to reach
inadequate	Not sufficient, not large enough
inclement	Rough, stormy, harsh
indentation	Cut, notch, deep recess, dent
ingenious	Showing cleverness, clever
ingest	To take in to be digested, eaten
insatiable	Unable to be satisfied
intact	Uninjured, kept whole, in one piece
intensified	To become stronger, to magnify
intertwine	To weave together

GLOSSARY

interweave	To place several items in a winding and zigzag pattern
invested	To put into, to spend much time and energy on something
magnificent	Extraordinarily fine, superb, splendid
mandatory	Containing a command, have to do
mustered	To call forth, to accumulate
nonetheless	However
observant	To see, perceive, or notice
perceive	To become aware of through senses
perception	Viewpoint, how you think about something or someone
perpendicular	Upright position at a right angle
pizzazz	Flair, dash, style
profusely	Pouring forth in a large amount
progressively	Going forward and onward in a slow, steady motion
recommendations	To advise a person, offer suggestions with advice
rejuvenate	Make new again, restore
reluctantly	Slowly with little desire
reminiscing	Recalling past experiences, thinking about the past
remnants	Small parts of, pieces
resilient	To adjust easily to change or misfortune
retrieve	To recover or regain, to find and fetch
ridicule	To laugh at or make fun of, mock or taunt

scurry   To move quickly from one place to another

shielded   Anything used or serving to protect, to help block

shimmied   Moving carefully, short careful movements, like army crawl

shrewd   Sharp in practical matters, clever

slither   To slip or glide along like a snake

spear   Like a weapon with a long wooden shaft with a sharp head

subsided   Settle, become quiet and content

succulent   Having fleshy tissue, juicy

summoned   Called

traction   The adhesive friction of a body, grip

turbulence   Full of commotion, wild, violently agitated

twirling   Rotate rapidly, spinning

ultimately   Last in the progression, at last

unpredictable   Unable to foretell the outcome, not knowing what will happen

vigilant   To be watchful in order to avoid danger

vigorously   Active force, with energy

yearned   To feel a longing or craving, long for

CPSIA information can be obtained at www.ICGtesting.com
Printed in the USA
LVOW020520121212

311195LV00005B/172/P